Titles in Series S852

Cinderella

Three Little Pigs

Goldilocks and the Three Bears

Jack and the beanstalk

Snow White and the Seven Dwarfs

The Ugly Duckling

Sleeping Beauty

Hansel and Gretel

The Gingerbread Man

Red Riding Hood

These titles are also available in two gift box sets

British Library Cataloguing in Publication Data
Murdock, Hy
   Hansel and Gretel.—(First fairy tales).
   I. Title   II. Waite, Bruce   III. Grimm, Jacob
   IV. Series
   823'.914[J]   PZ7
   ISBN 0-7214-9559-1

First edition
Published by Ladybird Books Ltd Loughborough Leicestershire UK
Ladybird Books Inc Lewiston Maine 04240 USA
© LADYBIRD BOOKS LTD MCMLXXXVII
Printed in England

Hansel and Gretel

written by HY MURDOCK
illustrated by BRUCE WAITE

Ladybird Books

Once upon a time a woodcutter and his wife lived in a cottage on the edge of the forest. The woodcutter had two children – a boy named Hansel and a girl named Gretel.

But the woodcutter's wife, who was the children's stepmother, didn't like children. The family was very poor and they were often hungry.

One night, when their food was nearly gone, the stepmother said, ''We must take the children into the forest and leave them.''

The woodcutter was sad. He loved his children — but there was no food for them and so he agreed.

Hansel and Gretel were so hungry that they lay awake in bed. They had heard what their stepmother had said. Gretel began to cry.

"Don't cry," said Hansel. "I'll save us."

He crept outside and quietly filled his pockets with small white pebbles which shone in the moonlight.

The next morning, their stepmother gave
Hansel and Gretel some bread to take with
them. The family set off into the forest
but Hansel walked slowly behind, dropping
pebbles from his pocket.

Deep in the forest the woodcutter made a
fire for his children and told them to stay by
it. ''We shall come back for you,'' he said.

Hansel and Gretel ate their bread and soon they went to sleep by the fire. When they woke, it was dark and they were afraid. Then Hansel said, "I can find the way back. I left a trail of pebbles! Look how they shine in the moonlight!"

The woodcutter was pleased to see them but their stepmother was very cross that they had found their way home.

It was not long before the stepmother made the woodcutter promise again that he would leave Hansel and Gretel in the forest. The children heard but this time the door was locked and Hansel couldn't creep out to collect any pebbles.

Next day, Hansel and Gretel took their pieces of bread and the woodcutter led them even deeper into the forest. Hansel walked slowly behind.

The woodcutter made a fire and again left
Hansel and Gretel in the forest. They went to
sleep and did not wake up until it was dark.

They knew they were lost but Hansel told
Gretel he had left a trail of breadcrumbs so
that they could find their way back.

They searched in the moonlight but couldn't
find the trail. The birds who lived in the
forest had eaten Hansel's crumbs.

In the morning the children wandered in the forest again. Suddenly they found a very strange cottage, made from delicious things like bread, cakes, sticks of sugar... chocolate...

They were so hungry that they broke off pieces to eat.

Then out came an ugly woman who said in a cackling voice, ''My dears! You are lost. Come and stay with me. I will give you food and look after you.'' The children were afraid but they went inside.

They didn't know that this old woman was really a wicked witch who liked to eat children.

But they soon found out!

The witch locked Hansel in a cage. ''I shall feed him until he is nice and fat and then I shall cook him in the oven,'' she cackled.

Every day the witch asked Hansel to poke his finger through the bar of the cage so that she could feel how fat he was. But clever Hansel held out a stick instead of his finger and the witch (who couldn't see very well) didn't know why he felt so thin.

One morning the witch was tired of waiting.
She made Gretel make a big fire in the oven.
Then the witch told her to climb inside to see if
it was hot enough. But Gretel said, ''Perhaps
you could get inside and see for yourself?''

As soon as the witch climbed into the oven,
Gretel slammed the door shut.

Gretel ran to let Hansel out of the cage. The children found jewels in the witch's cottage. Now they were rich!

When they returned home they found that their stepmother had gone. The woodcutter was overjoyed to see his children and they all lived happily ever after.